Good Night Engines

by Denise Dowling Mortensen

illustrated by Melissa Iwai

Clarion Books □ New York

Clarion Books
a Houghton Mifflin Company imprint
215 Park Avenue South, New York, NY 10003
Text copyright © 2003 by Denise Dowling Mortensen
Illustrations copyright © 2003 by Melissa Iwai

The illustrations were executed in acrylic paint.
The text was set in 26-point Cochin.

www.houghtonmifflinbooks.com

Printed in Singapore.

Library of Congress Cataloging-in-Publication Data
Mortensen, Denise Dowling.
Good night engines / by Denise Dowling Mortensen ; illustrated by Melissa Iwai.
p. cm.
Summary: Rhyming verses describe how a variety of vehicles, from locomotives to eighteen-wheelers
to automobiles, wind down for a night of rest.
ISBN 0-618-13537-5
[1. Vehicles—Fiction. 2. Bedtime—Fiction. 3. Stories in rhyme.] I. Iwai, Melissa, ill. II. Title.
PZ8.3.M842Go 2003
[E]—dc21   2002155215

TWP 10 9 8 7 6 5 4 3 2 1

To Erin, Brian, Andrew, Katie,
and my littlest engine, Patrick
—D. D. M.

For my mother
—M. I.

Locomotive whistle whine.
Engine thunders down the line.

6

Sunset glowing in the west.

Engine slowing,
wheels at rest.

Trucks with eighteen wheels below,
mighty engines in a row.

moon jumper dairy

Neon truck stop up ahead.
Big rigs rolling off to bed.

Jumbo jet plane
cleared to land.

15

Downward, roaring
turbofan.

17

Wheels on runway in a rush.
Grinding. Stopping. Resting.

Hush.

18

19

Fire engine, work is done.
To the station, end of run.

Scrubbed-down hoses,
shiny chrome.

Silent engine
safe at home.

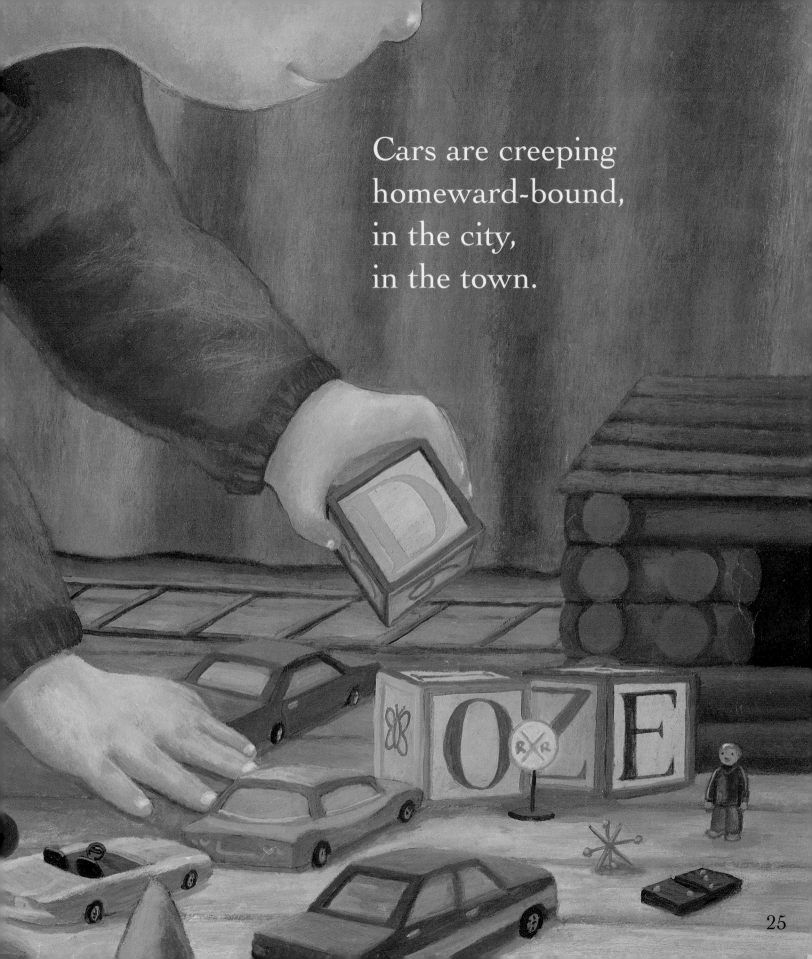

Cars are creeping
homeward-bound,
in the city,
in the town.

Engines humming,
stop and park.
Quiet. Resting.
Almost dark.

All the engines slumber deep.

Close your eyes
and go to sleep.

Turn off motor,
switch off light.

Tired engine . . .

. . . say good night.